THE DINOSAUR HUNTERS

THE CASEBOOK OF HARRIET GEORGE:
VOLUME 1

PATRICK SAMPHIRE

THE DINOSAUR HUNTERS

MARS, 1815

~

$\mathcal{H}$arriet George had been dressed as a boy for the last week, and she still wasn't sure her brother-in-law had noticed.

"The thing is, Harry old thing," the Honorable Bertrand Simpson said as he hunched morosely over his twelfth cup of tea that morning, "disguises are such dashed confusing things. Can't tell if a chap is a chap or, you know, another chap." He stirred his tea listlessly.

It had never been entirely clear to Harriet how her brother-in-law had managed to work his way up to the post of Inspector in the Tharsis City Police Service. As far as Harriet could tell, Bertrand had never solved a single case in his entire life.

Unfortunately, Harriet suspected that she wasn't the only one who had figured that out. It was the only reason she could think of as to why Bertrand had been given the job of capturing the Glass Phantom. The Glass Phantom had evaded police forces in France, Austria, Britain, and Chinese Mars. He'd helped himself to the Crown of Charlemagne from under the nose of Napoleon's Imperial Guard and had stolen the Orlov Diamond from the Imperial Scepter of Catherine the Great. No one with an ounce of common sense would risk their career tracking down such a notorious and difficult-to-catch jewel thief.

Which was why Bertrand, who wouldn't have recognized an ounce of common sense if it had fallen into his morning tea, had leapt on the offer like a piranha-mouse on a stray muffin.

Bertrand came from a good family – his father was the fifth Baron Heatherstone – but his family's estates on Earth had long ago been sold off to pay their debts. Bertrand's father had brought the family to Mars to seek his fortune on a new world, but it hadn't made any difference, and Bertrand scarcely had a penny to his name. In his position, he should have married a young lady with a good dowry. Instead, he'd married Harriet's older sister, Amy. If it hadn't been for Bertrand's job, Harriet was certain they would have starved within the year.

And then, five years ago, Harriet and Amy's parents had died, and Amy and Bertrand had taken Harriet in. She knew it had been hard for them, and she knew they'd given up a great deal for her. She owed them everything.

When Bertrand failed to catch the Glass Phantom, he would lose his job and it would be an absolute disaster for them all.

Harriet would *not* allow that to happen.

"You know, the Glass Phantom might not actually be in disguise," Harriet said, trying to cheer her brother-in-law up. "I mean, why would he?"

Bertrand groaned. "That makes it even worse. If he's not in disguise, how am I going to tell who he's not disguising himself as?"

Which, Harriet thought, summed up rather neatly why her brother-in-law never actually caught anyone.

To make matters worse, now that Harriet had turned sixteen, Amy was determined to make a good marriage for her, a prospect that Harriet regarded with complete horror. Within a year – two at the most – she would be expected to "come out" in Society, find a husband, and live the life *he* chose for her. She was already thoroughly fed up with the bother of being a girl, and this was the final straw. She'd never seen the point of sewing or playing the pianoforte or endless, tedious social visits to neighbors, and what was more, she had very little interest in young gentlemen. If she was entirely honest, very few young gentlemen showed any interest in her, either. But Amy had set her heart on Harriet marrying well. She seemed to think she owed it to their late parents, and Harriet couldn't live off Bertrand's generosity forever, particularly if he lost his job.

Which left Harriet with only one option: she would

have to solve the case for Bertrand, and she would have to prove to her sister that she could support herself without a husband.

The dinosaur hunt was the perfect opportunity.

It had all started a month ago.

Bertrand had been tootling happily away, failing to put away criminals but generally not getting in anyone's way, when a courier had arrived by Mars-ship from Earth with a warning: the Glass Phantom was travelling to Mars to steal the Countess von Krakendorff's famous ruby necklace.

The British military force had been shattered following Napoleon's overwhelming victory at Trafalgar, leaving Britain unable to interfere with the Emperor's conquests of Europe, Africa, and North America and his ongoing assault on South America, but its intelligence gathering remained robust. The British-Martian Intelligence Service had thought the warning reliable enough to pass onto the Tharsis City Police, before it eventually landed in the eager if inept lap of the Honorable Bertrand Simpson.

Harriet didn't know whether her brother-in-law had volunteered for the assignment or whether he'd *been* volunteered, and Bertrand himself seemed unsure, but the job had become his, and no one else wanted to get anywhere near it.

Bertrand had been sure that the Glass Phantom would strike at one of the many balls and parties that took place in the great hanging ballrooms of Tharsis City, the capital of British Mars. Tharsis City had been built among the ruins of the Ancient Martian civilization, on the slopes of the extinct volcano, Tharsis Mons. Here, where the cliffs fell away to the plains below, the first Martian explorers had found gigantic buildings made of unbreakable emerald jutting from the cliffs and suspended from above like strange fruit, one side open to the air to catch the first rays of the morning sun. As the city had grown, latticeworks of iron and glass had been built across the open walls, and the vast spaces had been turned into a series of glittering ballrooms where guests could dance until dawn.

Bertrand had had half the Tharsis City police in attendance, watching every guest, but the Glass Phantom hadn't showed. As the days passed and the Glass Phantom made no appearance, Bertrand's superiors had begun to believe that the tip-off was a hoax and had started to ask pointed questions about the use of funds.

Maybe someone else would have given up and tried to salvage something of their career. But not Bertrand. If there was one thing that could be said about her brother-in-law, Harriet thought, it was that he was stubborn. When the countess had announced that she would be travelling to the Great Wall of Cyclopia to observe a dinosaur hunt, Bertrand had decided to accompany her. And that was when Harriet had conceived her plan to save them all.

So, a week later, Bertrand and Harriet had found themselves on Harrison Airfield, ready to board the expedition airship flying west to the Great Wall.

The airfield had been built a few miles north of Tharsis City, around the flank of the mountain, just below where the dragon path from Earth terminated. When the Mars-ships floated down from the void on the vast current of wind, twin mechanical arms reached out to pull the ships down to the docking bay. Harriet had never ridden on a Mars-ship – she'd never actually traveled further than a couple of hours beyond Tharsis City – but she'd watched the Mars-ships descend and then lift off again, carried by the powerful wind on their journeys back to Earth. An airship might not be a Mars-ship but it was the next best thing for someone who'd never travelled anywhere.

One day I'm flying on one of those, she swore to herself. *I'm going to go everywhere.*

The expedition airship was tethered to the ground in front of them. A platform had been lowered from the center of the crew compartment, and mechanics were attaching the two massive, flat springs that would drive the propellers. Harriet noticed that the airship's balloon was covered in armored panels.

Nothing to worry about there then. Just because none of the other airships feel the need for armored panels...

"Are you sure Amy is happy about this?" Bertrand

asked for the third time, his brow wrinkling, as they climbed the sloping platform into the belly of the airship. "It doesn't *seem* like the kind of thing she'd approve of."

"Of course!" Harriet said, feeling slightly guilty about lying. As far as Amy knew, Harriet was spending a month with her distant cousin Florentia.

Oh well. Amy should have known better. The idea that Harriet would voluntarily spend more than an hour listening to Florentia witter on about fashion was beyond absurd.

"Come on," Harriet said. "Let's find our cabins."

IT WAS THE MIDDLE OF AUTUMN ON BRITISH MARS, AND the shimmer-stream migration had begun. At this time of year, the prevailing winds shifted and rivers of startlingly blue shimmer-stream pollen lifted from the slopes above Tharsis City and were swept east toward the wilderness. As the airship rose through the semi-sentient pollen, Harriet felt like she was inside a great leviathan, ascending through the waters of the Valles Marineris to breach the surface. It made her feel free for the first time in years.

Even with the airship's powerful, spring-driven engines, the trip from Tharsis to the Great Wall of Cyclopia would take almost a week, and for most of that time they would be passing over unbroken wilderness, unsettled and unexplored since the days of the

Ancient Martian Empire. The airship would skirt the northern border of Turkish Mars, then follow the coast of the Elysium Sea before cutting inland across the rolling Hesperian wilderness.

They picked up more passengers on the way: a middle-aged couple called Mr. and Mrs. Patterson at New Hibernia, then two slightly drunk young men at Port Sabis on the north-western border of Turkish Mars. Now the airship was beating its way over the wild lands toward the Great Wall of Cyclopia and the Amenthes Peninsula behind it, where they would find the dinosaurs.

There were thirteen of them in the party, not including the captain and crew of the airship, and Harriet had to admit that if the Glass Phantom was part of this group, he was doing an excellent job of hiding it.

"We don't actually know that the Glass Phantom is a man, do we?" Harriet said thoughtfully, as she watched their companions.

The countess was sitting, straight-backed, with her admirer, Baron de Sorville, and her maid, Maria. The Pattersons were talking with a portly, elderly man, Major Beaumont, to Mrs. Patterson's apparent displeasure. The two young men were drinking loudly next to a wide window, and another shabby young man, who had introduced himself to Harriet as Neville Seymour, a young journalist from *The Tharsis Times,* sat by himself, scribbling in a notebook with a frayed autoquill. His employer, the newspaper proprietor Sir

Angus Cameron, was resting in his cabin, as was the last member of their party, the renowned natural historian Professor Riemann.

Harriet gazed at Neville Seymour with displeasure. She hadn't planned for a journalist to be on board. Her plan to prove that she could support herself had been to write up the dinosaur hunt and Bertrand's subsequent capture of the Glass Phantom and sell it as an exclusive to one of the newspapers. Seymour's presence threw an unwanted spanner in her plans.

Bertrand swung around to face Harriet, his mouth falling open in horror. "You think the Glass Phantom is a *woman*?"

"Why not?" Harriet said. "It would make perfect sense. No one would be looking for a woman." As far as most men were concerned, women had neither the wits nor the courage for such activities. Harriet had often wondered whether a life of crime might be worth pursuing. "She'd hardly be noticed."

"But... But... A *female*?" Bertrand sputtered. "*Stealing?*"

"You obviously don't know Amy as well as you think you do," Harriet said. "She spent most of her childhood filching pastries from the kitchen."

"That's not the same," Bertrand said, reddening.

"Anyway, he might not be," Harriet said.

Bertrand slumped. "At least we know no one's stolen the jewels yet." He rubbed his eyes. "No one's gone near the countess's cabin without her since she wore her necklace at dinner last night." He yawned. "Not sure how long I'm going to be able to keep it up."

He straightened in his seat, stretching and wincing. Harriet knew how he felt. She'd spent most of the night here with him, only giving up and returning to her cabin a couple of hours before dawn.

Someone cleared their throat directly behind them. Harriet had to grab the arms of her chair to stop from jumping in surprise. Bertrand wasn't so lucky. He jerked forward, spilling his tea. Harriet swung around to see the wispy-haired Professor Riemann standing only a foot away.

"Please accept my apologies, Mr. Simpson," the professor said. "I did not mean to startle you."

"Ah." Bertrand stumbled to his feet, almost tripping over their low table. "Professor Riemann. We, er, didn't see you there. Have you been there long?"

"Not long." If he'd heard them talking about the countess's emeralds, he gave no sign of it. Something about his pale gaze made Harriet shiver. He indicated the seat opposite her. "May I?"

"Of course," Bertrand said, reddening. "Rude of me."

"This," the professor said, nodding toward the window as he lowered himself slowly into the chair, "is where they found the remains of the Artherton expedition."

Harriet cleared her throat. "The Artherton expedition?"

"1758," the professor said. "Sidney Artherton. He

resolved to find an overland route from Tharsis to Cyclopia. The remains of his expedition were discovered in the wilderness just below where we are now. Most of the members of the expedition were never recovered, but Artherton and his assistant, Connolly, were found here. Their bodies were entirely crystalized. It was a most peculiar case and it was quite a sensation in the newspapers at the time." A look of distaste crossed the professor's face. "Of course, we now know it was the work of the weaver beetle, which turns its hosts' bodies into chrysalises, but at the time all sorts of lurid theories were put forward.

"It was a shame." His face twisted again, although to Harriet it looked more like contempt than sympathy for the dead men. "They were no more than twenty miles from the Great Wall. Some theorize that the expedition actually made it to the Wall and was on its way back when disaster overtook them, but there is no evidence to support that theory." He smiled thinly. "I would strongly recommend that you do not find yourselves alone in the wilderness. There are many hazards for the unwary." His bland eyes didn't waver from Harriet. She clenched her hands into fists under the table. Was he *threatening* them? Why would he do that? Then he blinked, breaking the gaze. "We should be able to see the Great Wall from here."

"What do you say, Harry old thing?" Bertrand said. "Fancy a glimpse?"

Harriet's heart sped up as she nodded. There were few sights on Mars as famously magnificent as the

Great Wall of Cyclopia. The dragon tombs of Lunae
Planum held wonders of technology scarcely dreamed
of, and the buildings of Tharsis City outshone
anything from Venice to Beijing, but in terms of sheer,
impossible scale, the Great Wall was unmatched. It
stretched over seven hundred and fifty miles and was
at least three hundred yards high, cutting off the entire
Amenthes Peninsula from the Hesperian landmass.
Behind the Wall lay three hundred thousand square
miles of wilderness, and in that wilderness roamed
those ancient reptiles, the dinosaurs.

Harriet stepped onto the viewing platform at the
front of the airship with Bertrand at her side. At first
she couldn't even make out the Wall, it was so large. It
was more like the line of the horizon stretching as far
as the eye could see and rising hundreds of feet from
the tangled wilderness, as though the planet had
simply been cut in two, and one half had slipped
down, exposing the bedrock.

Storm hawks circled over the Wall, their enormous
wings drawing tiny crackles of lightning from the clear
air as they searched for their prey. One of the birds
folded its wings as Harriet watched, plunging down
into the wilderness far below. Released lightning
flashed beneath the canopy.

Out here, the wind was cold and the beat of the
airship's spring-powered propellers felt like a giant
pulse thumping through Harriet. She felt a sudden
urge to leap from the balcony, her arms spread wide
like the storm hawks' wings, and soar into the sky.

She'd never felt so free in Tharsis City. She realized she was grinning madly.

"One must believe that Atherton and Connolly would have been able to see the Wall from where they fell," Professor Riemann said from Harriet's shoulder. He was supporting himself on his walking stick with its silver handle shaped like a dragon's head, complete with sharp teeth. "It is a shame they did not return, because their insights into Martian flora and fauna might have advanced our knowledge of natural history by decades."

"Also, they wouldn't have been dead," Harriet added cheerily. "So there would have been that."

The professor waved his hand dismissively.

"Is that the damned Wall at last?" a loud voice called from the doorway behind Harriet. "About time."

She glanced back to see one of the young men poke his head out. Their names were Eric Matfield and James Renton. Harriet had never bothered to remember which name was attached to which man. They were both too young to be the Glass Phantom, and as far as Harriet was concerned, there was nothing else of interest about either of them.

The young man stepped out, wincing in the sunlight.

"We will land within the hour," Professor Riemann said.

As if in echo, the airship captain appeared in the doorway. "We're approaching the Wall," he said. "We must close off the viewing platform. Several species of pterosaur roost near the top of the Wall, and some of the larger creatures have been known to attack approaching airships."

"Ha!" Renton, or possibly Matfield, said. "Just our luck. Stuck for a week on this blasted flying balloon, then torn out of the sky by some wretched flying lizard."

"The airship is quite safe," the captain assured him. "The balloon is reinforced and impervious to their claws or beaks. But anyone on the viewing platform might be vulnerable."

"You know we're out here hunting dinosaurs?" the young man said with a laugh. "We're not exactly scared of a few flapping reptiles. Wouldn't mind taking a potshot on the way past, though."

"If you please," the captain insisted, holding open the door.

"We should get back," Bertrand whispered into Harriet's ear. "I shouldn't leave the countess's room unwatched. Not until we've caught the confounded thief."

With a suppressed sigh, Harriet turned away.

Inside, the ship's automatic servants were lined up in a glittering metal row. Sir Angus Cameron, the newspaper proprietor, had emerged from his cabin and appeared to be haranguing the young journalist, Neville Seymour.

"Might I suggest that you pack whatever you wish to take from the airship?" the captain said, as he closed the door to the viewing platform. "The expedition has a base set up in the Wall, and those of you going on the hunt itself will descend to the ground this evening. The automatic servants are available to help, should anyone wish to make use of them."

"You go," Bertrand said in a quiet voice. "Pack my stuff too, if you don't mind. I want to keep an eye on the countess's room until I know she's got her baggage."

Harriet hadn't brought much with her, just the few changes of boy's clothes that she'd been able to lay her hands on without raising Amy's suspicions. Harriet had seen the way Matfield and Renton had sneered at her when they'd realized she only had a couple of outfits, but there were few things Harriet cared less about than their opinion, and anyway, they'd reserved most of their contempt for Neville Seymour, who'd been wearing the same jacket since they'd boarded. Harriet had almost felt sorry for him, even though he was her rival.

Within five minutes Harriet had packed her and Bertrand's trunks and handed them off to the automatic servants.

"Anything?" she asked as she rejoined Bertrand.

He shook his head. "They're all in their own cabins."

Harriet hadn't expected the Glass Phantom to strike on the airship. If she'd been the thief, she would have waited until the dinosaur hunt was underway and everyone's attention was distracted.

"I think it's that Baron de Sorville," Bertrand said. "He's always hanging around the countess."

"Maybe," Harriet said. She'd be disappointed if it was. She didn't think the Glass Phantom would be so obvious.

"I've a good mind to arrest him right now."

"On what charge?"

Bertrand glared around the lounge. "Just ... because. Come on, Harry. Don't you think he looks guilty?"

The door to the lounge opened, and the countess emerged, arm-in-arm with Baron de Sorville and followed by her maid, Maria.

The Great Wall was approaching, filling the forward windows like a bank of storm clouds. The airship had been descending for the last hour, and now the Wall loomed dark and massive ahead of them. This close, Harriet could see cracks and openings in the smooth rock of the Wall.

"Why are we coming in so low?" Harriet asked. They were a good hundred yards below the top of the Wall.

"The winds sweep up the side of the Wall," said Major Beaumont, his heavy jowls shaking as he puffed out the words. "Too high up and the turbulence can throw an airship out of the sky."

"You've done this trip before, then?" Bertrand asked.

"My fifth hunt," the major huffed. "Winged a gnarly old Triceratops my first time out. Trying to bag the beast ever since. Magnificent horns and shield on it. Plan to mount them over my fireplace. Ha!"

Mrs. Patterson sniffed. "I always thought the Triceratops terribly common. Our neighbor, Mr. Casson, has a Triceratops head."

"Not like this one, madam," Major Beaumont snorted. "Not like this one, I assure you."

The airship juddered in the air. Its propellers whined.

"What is it?" Mrs. Patterson demanded, turning to her husband. "What's happening, Harold?"

Mr. Patterson shrank down. His face had turned white.

"It's the wind," the major said. "It's lifting us."

Through the windows, the Great Wall seemed to be falling away, as though crumbling at its base. The airship shook and turned in the air as the captain fought to keep it level.

"You might want to hold onto something," the major said.

Harriet steadied herself on a nearby table. They were ascending more and more rapidly. She swallowed to stop her eardrums popping.

"This is where it gets interesting!" the major shouted. A moment later, the Wall fell away below and the airship was flung up into the sky, spinning around like a loose top. Harriet grabbed tighter to the table as the violent motion threatened to throw her from her feet. Bertrand sprawled to his knees, and he wasn't the only one. For a moment, it seemed as though their airship was tumbling free, like a tossed stone, arcing through the air to inevitably fall back to earth. Then the airship's propellers gained traction and slowly the airship steadied. When Harriet pulled herself over to the windows, she saw that they had passed over the Great Wall. Beyond, the Amenthes Peninsula stretched away further than she could see, rising and falling in a rumpled quilt of green and cut through by glittering blue rivers and lakes. Far in the haze of the horizon, hills rose.

"My apologies, ladies and gentlemen." The captain's voice emerged from a speaking tube in the ceiling. "The winds are particularly strong today. We'll be descending to our docking point in a couple of minutes. Enjoy your hunt!"

The far side of the Great Wall was quite different to the side they'd approached from. Enormous elliptical openings dotted the Wall every few hundred yards, and the openings themselves must have been a good fifty yards across. As their airship descended past one, Harriet caught sight of an airship moored inside.

"We're not the only ones here!" she said.

"Indeed not," Professor Riemann said. "The Great Wall was once inhabited, thousands of years ago, and it is riddled with chambers and passages. There are several teams of archaeologists working within it."

"Can't see the blasted point," Matfield, or Renton, said. "Why spend your life poking around some moldy old wall when you could be shooting dinosaurs on the other side?"

"The point, young man, is artifacts," said the professor.

Renton, or Matfield, snorted. "Thought they were all in the dragon tombs in the desert. That's what they told us when we went up to Lunae City anyway."

The professor lifted his chin. "It is true that most Ancient Martian artifacts have been recovered from the dragon tombs of Lunae Planum. The dry desert air preserves them, and it seems the Ancient Martians delighted in filling their tombs with their greatest mechanisms. Here, storms batter the Great Wall through much of the year and the air is humid so most artifacts have decayed, but I understand that there are still some to be found deep in the Wall, and those are valuable."

"Valuable?" Mrs. Patterson laughed. "As though those primitives could have anything worth finding."

Those primitives, Harriet thought, had built a wall big enough to swallow any of Earth's cities without a trace. Their artifacts were basis of every technological advancement in the last hundred years. Those *primitives* had had a civilization greater than any on Earth.

"Ah!" Major Beaumont called. "Looks like we're here!"

The airship had come to a halt, hovering in front of one of the wide, elliptical openings in the Wall. Inside, a line of bright lights burned. The airship turned, and within minutes, it had docked inside the cavernous opening. With a last sigh, the propellers disengaged. The automatic servants moved forward to crank down the gangway in the middle of the lounge. Humid air rolled over Harriet, and she took a deep breath. This high above the wilderness, all she could catch was a slight hint of the rich, damp, spicy smells of vegetation below, but even so, it tasted wonderful. *I could live out here*, she thought. Compared to the claustrophobic staleness of Tharsis City with people pressed in on every side, watching everything she did, this was freedom. *Dinosaurs don't care how you dress. The storm hawks don't care if you speak out of turn.*

The gangway hit the floor of the docking bay with a clang, revealing a single figure outlined by the landing lights. The man was tall and broad shouldered, carrying the kind of muscle only seen on those who grew up in the higher gravity of Earth. If Harriet had had to guess, she would have put him at a good ten years older than Bertrand.

"Who the devil are you?" the major demanded, stepping onto the gangway. "Where's Perkins? He leads the hunts."

"Mr. Perkins," the man said, "was killed by a Megalosaurus last month. My name is Stanley Scott. I'm his replacement. You must be Major Beaumont."

The major harrumphed. "Always thought Perkins was more careful than that."

Harriet tried to catch Bertrand's eye. Scott was old enough to be the Glass Phantom, and he'd turned up here unexpectedly. But Bertrand was too busy gaping around the cavern.

"The automatic servants will bring your luggage," Scott said, pacing back and forth with a compressed-air gun slung over one shoulder – *prowling*, Harriet thought. "Rooms have been prepared for you in the Wall. All of them have excellent views out over the peninsula. I must caution you, however, that you may not stray from the lighted areas. The Great Wall is a restricted area, by agreement of the Martian governments. There are alarms at all exits, and we are only allowed to use this section for the hunts on the condition that everyone remains within at all times."

He dropped his gun into both hands. "This is for your own safety. The interior of the Wall is dark, crumbling, and dangerous. *Things* from the wilderness have taken up residence in places. It would be highly dangerous to stray.

"For those of you who are intending to take part in the hunt itself, we will be descending to our camp at the base of the Wall this evening. I've been tracking a pack of Coelophysis for the last week. They should prove an excellent introduction to the hunt. They are fast, vicious, and intelligent, but they are small and not an enormous threat if you keep your heads. If you need to borrow weapons, please talk to me. Those of you who will not be hunting will have the opportunity to observe dinosaurs in safety from our viewing lodge tomorrow." He nodded. "Thank you. Be ready in two hours."

One of the automatic servants led Harriet and Bertrand down a hallway that had been cut from the slick rock of the Wall toward their rooms. Harriet had no idea how the passageways had been lit when the Wall had been built, thousands of years ago – they passed a stairway that descended into unrelieved blackness – but friction lamps, powered by coiled springs, had been set at intervals along the hallway they were using.

Scott was a complication she didn't need. *Another potential suspect to add to an airship full.* He didn't *seem* like a jewel thief. But wouldn't that be the point? Anyway, so far *no one* had seemed like a jewel thief.

Harriet's room was the third along. As the automatic servant placed her trunk beside her bed, she made her way across to the wide window of her room and peered out. Far below, the green wilderness stretched to the horizon. Harriet squinted to see if she could catch a glimpse of the mighty reptiles that roamed the peninsula, but from this high she couldn't spot anything. She hurried across to her trunk to dig out her spyglass.

The countess had made it quite clear that she wouldn't be taking part in the actual hunt. She'd be waiting for the next day to fly out to the viewing lodge and observe the dinosaurs in comfort. That meant Harriet and Bertrand would have to stay too. It made Harriet want to shout in frustration. She'd come here to catch the Glass Phantom, but now she was here, all she wanted to do was get down there into the wilderness. Not to hunt the dinosaurs, but to walk on the same ground as them, smell the same smells, feel the same rain on her back. Be as free.

She wished the Glass Phantom would just get on with it.

A scream echoed from the corridor outside. Harriet froze, her heart suddenly pounding.

Well. That was quicker than she'd expected. Unless something horrific had crawled out of the Wall. She shivered and wished she'd brought a weapon.

The door burst open, making Harriet's heart leap again, and Bertrand appeared. His hair was disheveled and his eyes wide. "Come on, Harry!"

Harriet took off in pursuit. They dashed down the long hallway and into the docking bay. Most of the rest of the party were already there, clustered around the countess, although Harriet noticed that the young men, Matfield and Renton, were missing, and Major Beaumont was only just arriving behind them, his wide face red. The Baron de Sorville was hanging solicitously on the countess's arm, and the countess's maid, Maria, hovered white-faced behind her.

"What is it?" Bertrand demanded. "What's happened?"

"My jewels!" the countess said. "My necklace! It is gone."

For a moment, Bertrand just stood there, his mouth gaping open.

Harriet nudged him. "You're up."

"What?"

"You're a policeman. Remember?"

Bertrand blinked. "Ah. Yes." He cleared his throat and peered around the gathered group. "Ladies and gentlemen. If you please?"

Faces turned toward Bertrand and his face reddened. "Ah…"

"What do you have to say for yourself, young man?" the countess demanded. "Do you know where my jewels are?"

"I am very sorry to inform you," Bertrand said, his voice shaking slightly, "that your necklace has been stolen by the Glass Phantom."

"Don't be ridiculous," Matfield, or possibly Renton, snorted. "You're making up stories."

"I am an inspector in the Tharsis City Police Force," Bertrand said. "I know what I'm talking about. It was my job to find the Glass Phantom and prevent the theft of the necklace."

"And how's that going?" the other young man said with a laugh.

Bertrand reddened further.

Damnation! Harriet had hoped they would uncover the Glass Phantom before he or she struck so Bertrand would never find himself in this situation. Now that he was, he was making a hash of it.

"You need to search them," she hissed.

Bertrand glanced around. "What?"

"You have to search them and their luggage."

Bertrand's jaw dropped. "I can't search the ladies!" He frowned. Then his eyes lit up. "Perhaps you…"

"No," Harriet said firmly. To do that, she would have to reveal herself as a girl. It would completely spoil her disguise and ruin her plan to save them. It wasn't an option. "Ask the ladies to search each other."

In any case, Harriet didn't believe for a second that they would find the stolen necklace so easily. The Glass Phantom had eluded Napoleon's spies and half the police forces of Earth. He – or she – wouldn't have the jewels hidden in their luggage or stashed in a pocket.

And she was right. She and Bertrand spent over two hours carrying out a thorough search of the airship and their rooms in the Wall, but to no avail. The necklace had vanished.

"The problem is," Harriet said, as she helped Bertrand repack the last trunk, "the thief might not even have the necklace anymore. They might just as easily have tossed it out the airship or into one of those dark staircases in the Wall to retrieve it later."

"I don't even know how he did it, Harry," Bertrand said "I mean, I *know* no one went into the countess's cabin without her being present."

"Except her maid," Harriet said.

"You think it was the maid?"

Harriet shrugged. "Could have been. Or it could have been someone else entirely. The Glass Phantom is clever."

"But I'm not." Bertrand drooped. "We're not going to manage this, are we? I know what will happen if I come back empty-handed and the Glass Phantom gets away again. I'll be finished. I'm just not clever enough for this."

"It doesn't matter," Harriet said. "I'll help, and our

thief isn't going anywhere. He's stuck in the Wall like the rest of us."

"Are you done?" the major called across the docking bay. "Can we get on with the dashed hunt now?"

Well, Harriet corrected herself. *Maybe not stuck in the Wall. Maybe stuck out among the ravening dinosaurs instead.*

"Come on," Harriet said. "We can do this. Just keep asking questions. We'll find your thief in the end. I know it."

Bertrand sighed. "If you say so, Harry." He raised his voice and called across the bay. "Lady Krakendorff. Might we have a word with you in private?"

The countess gave Bertrand a long, cool look, then slowly made her way across the docking bay.

"I am not accustomed," she said, as she seated herself in a winged armchair that had been brought down from the airship, "to being summoned like a common *servant*."

Bertrand and Harriet seated themselves opposite her.

"My apologies, my lady," Bertrand said. "But we must ask you some questions if we are to recover your stolen jewelry. Could you tell us when you last saw your necklace?"

The countess lifted her chin. "I took it off after dinner last night. Since then, it has been locked in a strongbox in my cabin. There is only one key, and I keep it on my person at all times."

Bertrand gave Harriet a pained look. She knew that look. It was the one that said Bertrand had come to the end of his ideas. Harriet jumped in before Bertrand could dry up altogether.

"Did you notice anyone loitering around your cabin or showing particular interest in you?"

The countess looked away. "I am accustomed to particular interest. When one occupies the station that I do, such attention is my due."

Harriet gritted her teeth and kept the polite smile on her face. "Perhaps you could tell us about the Baron de Sorville."

"A dear friend. We met last year at the Congress of Vienna, when Europe surrendered to that monster, Napoleon. De Sorville lost his estates in France to the monster a decade earlier and had been living in Vienna."

A perfect place for the Glass Phantom to select his next victim, Harriet thought. Despite the surrender of Europe, the Congress of Vienna had hosted dozens of glittering balls and fashionable salons, and anyone who was anyone had been there. Harriet had seen many of the events reported in *The Tharsis Times*.

"And your maid, my lady?" Bertrand said. "Have you had her long?"

The countess sniffed. "Maria? She has been with me for three months. I retained her when my previous maid refused to travel to Mars with me. I have no time for such weak-willed creatures. Maria came to me with *excellent* references. I will not have you suspect her, do you understand? She is most loyal."

Bertrand cleared his throat awkwardly. "I don't mean to be rude, but isn't she a little old to be a lady's maid?"

"I cannot abide simpering youths, and I will not be attended to by one of those *mechanisms*." She flicked a dismissive hand at the automatic servants standing nearby.

"Thank you, my lady," Bertrand said. "I think we've got all we need."

"Very well," the countess said. "I expect you to find my necklace forthwith. I will not tolerate being robbed. It is quite beneath me."

"I don't like it, Harry," Bertrand said, as the countess made her way back to the gathering. "A new friend, a new maid, and a new guide for the hunt, not to mention all the rest of the party. What am I supposed to do with so many suspects?"

"How about the airship crew?" Harriet said.

"At least we can rule them out. I had them investigated before we departed. They've all been flying for the Imperial Martian Airship Company for years. None of them could be the Glass Phantom."

Harriet took her brother-in-law's hand. He was shaking. "We'll find him," she said.

She just didn't know how.

⌁

THEY DESCENDED TO THE GROUND BELOW THE WALL AS evening began to close in. Fireflowers were bursting into flame in the dense vegetation below, winking like orange stars as the heat from the brief fires lifted their pollen into the air.

The camp was in a wide clearing at the foot of the Wall, surrounded by tall hedges of stranglethorn. By the time the airship settled in the clearing, the sun was already dipping beneath the hills to the west, and the tall, spiky trees were throwing long, reaching shadows over the camp. The countess, her maid, and the Baron de Sorville had stayed behind in the Wall, but the rest of the party had continued on, and Harriet and Bertrand had followed. The maid and the baron were certainly suspects, but most of the party would be on the hunt, and Harriet figured they could cover more of them this way.

A semicircle of tents had been set up some distance back from a large, unlit bonfire. A single larger tent stood on the far side. As they trooped down into the camp, Stanley Scott beckoned them all over to the bonfire. A series of wooden benches had been arranged around it.

"We will begin the hunt at dawn," he said, kneeling down to set light to the fire with an auto-flint. "The hedges will prevent any dinosaur incursion, but predators do hunt close to the Wall. I must ask you not to leave the safety of the campsite during the night. I would prefer that you all survived the hunt. It's not good for business if any of our customers are eaten.

Now, please take your ease. The automatic servants will bring the evening meal in an hour."

"Well, Harry," Bertrand said as they settled themselves onto a bench. "What do you think?"

The rest of the party were seating themselves, Mrs. Patterson with a look of intense distaste as she lowered herself onto the rough wood. The two young men, Matfield and Renton, had found a bottle of whiskey and were sharing it on the far side of the fire.

"I think we need to question people. Find out a bit more about what they're doing here."

"You don't think the Glass Phantom will have a good cover story?"

"Of course he will," Harriet said. "But maybe it will be a little too good." She shrugged. The Glass Phantom would have been planning this for months. He'd have everything covered. The only thing that he wouldn't have planned for, she thought grimly, was how desperate she was. She *had* to uncover him or her family would be ruined.

Bertrand cleared his throat. "Ladies and gentlemen. I truly regret having to interrupt your evening, but I fear I must ask you all some questions. Perhaps you would be kind enough to let me know how you came to be on this expedition?" He looked around the circle. "Mr. Matfield and Mr. Renton, is it? Perhaps we could start with you. What brings you here?"

The first young man snorted. "Not really sure what business it is of yours, but we don't have anything to hide. Renton, ah, came into some money, didn't you, old fellow? So we've been taking a tour of Mars. We've been sky leaping in the air forests of Patagonian Mars, we rode the Red Needle in Turkish Mars—"

"And caused a scandal in New Guangzhou," Renton added, with a snigger.

"Now we thought we'd top it off with a bit of a hunt. Haven't blown your whole fortune yet, have we?" Matfield said to his friend.

"Where exactly did this money come from?" Harriet asked.

"Now, that really isn't any of your business," Matfield said. "So unless you plan to arrest us" – he raised his whiskey – "your health."

And suddenly coming into a mysterious fortune wasn't at all suspicious, was it? Harriet thought. She snorted to herself. But they were both still too young to be the Glass Phantom.

"You already know why I'm here," Major Beaumont said. "Been trying to bag that blasted Triceratops of mine for five years. He'd be able to confirm," the major said, nodding across to where their guide, Stanley Scott, sat cleaning a large rifle, "if he weren't new."

Conveniently, Harriet thought.

"You are in my notes, Major," the guide said, looking up. "Mr. Perkins left excellent notes about all our clients."

Notes, but no actual proof that this was the same man.

"I'll be leaving at first light to track the creature,"

the major said. "I'm going to damned well get it this year. Making a fool out of me."

"Ah," Bertrand said. "I'm not sure I can allow that."

The major puffed out his cheeks. "Not sure how you're going to stop me, young man."

"Sir Angus," Harriet interjected. The newspaper proprietor looked up, frowning. "What brings you here?"

"The hunt," he snapped. "What do you think? Not here for my health. Seymour here" – he waved a contemptuous hand at the reporter sitting next to him – "is going to write it up for my paper. Not good for much else. But now it looks like you've got a proper story on your hands, eh, boy? See if you can avoid making a hash of it."

Neville Seymour reddened, and Harriet felt a pang of sympathy, which she quickly pushed away. This was *her* story and her chance. Seymour was an obstacle. If he did mess it up, she would be in a prime position to sell her own story. And she'd have an inside angle with Bertrand.

Sir Angus was a public figure. She'd seen his picture in his own newspaper often enough. Unless he'd been darting off to Earth to nab jewels in between running his newspaper, he wasn't a suspect either.

"And Mr. and Mrs. Patterson?" Bertrand said.

Mrs. Patterson straightened. "Mrs. Casson's husband brought back a Triceratops head from this hunt last year."

"Casson was on my list," Stanley Scott confirmed.

"A Triceratops, a couple of Troodon, and a juvenile Apatosaurus."

"*As* I said. It is my intention that Harold should shoot a Tyrannosaurus rex. That will put Mrs. Casson in her place."

Her husband gripped his compressed-air gun with white fingers. "Yes, dear."

"Tyrannosaurus rexes are rare," Stanley Scott said. "I haven't seen one here for nearly a year."

"That," Mrs. Patterson said, "is precisely the point. I see no benefit in slaughtering a *common* dinosaur."

"Which just leaves you, Professor Riemann," Bertrand said. "If you'll forgive me, I wouldn't have marked you as a hunter."

The professor was an elderly, frail-looking man who had to lean on his dragon-headed walking stick to move about.

"I've read about you, haven't I?" Harriet said. "Something about dinosaurs. Not hunting, though. There was an article about you in *The Tharsis Times*."

The professor looked displeased. "An inaccurate piece, no doubt. I do not read such things."

Sir Angus Cameron stiffened, cheeks flushing, and glared at Professor Riemann. "How dare you? *The Tharsis Times* is the best newspaper on all Mars!"

"A poor boast." The professor pulled off his glasses and polished them on his sleeve.

The sun had finally set behind the western hills and the wash of red was fading from the dusk sky. The crackling bonfire had deepened the shadows around the camp to blackness, so Harriet couldn't see beyond the circle of hunters.

"You are correct, though, young man," the professor said to Harriet. "You may be aware that the bones of creatures similar to dinosaurs have recently been found in the rocks on Earth. I have developed a framework of comparison to see if the brutes are related. I intend to carry out such observations as would establish whether they are same species."

"I thought everyone knew they were," Harriet said.

The professor peered down at her. "It is not as simple as superficial observations might suggest. After all, if you were to simply observe the skeletons of native Martians, you might conclude that, other than their great height, they are human."

"But they are!"

"A ridiculous, fashionable notion. They are savages and cannot possibly be related to real people."

Harriet felt her jaw grinding. But before she could fire back, the undergrowth behind the tall, stranglethorn hedge shook and an enormous roar sounded, stilling the nighttime sounds and sending a shiver running up her spine.

"What's that?" Mr. Patterson demanded, clutching his gun to his chest. "What is it?"

Scott didn't look up. "Medium-sized theropod would be my guess. Ceratosaurus, or something similar. It's smelled the food cooking in the kitchen. Don't worry. It can't reach us through the stranglethorn hedge."

"We should shoot it!" Matfield wobbled slightly as he rose to his feet, his bottle of whiskey still in one hand. "Better way to start the hunt than whatever pack of rats you've got lined up for us tomorrow."

"Not at night. Even if you could see it before it saw you, it won't be the only thing out there."

Matfield sneered as he took his seat again.

The food arrived from the kitchen, brought on trays by the automatic servants, who moved smoothly and nearly soundlessly on well-oiled springs and cogs. Above the crackling of the fire, Harriet could hear strange cries and crashings in the wilderness beyond the camp, and once a loud, desperate trumpeting wail. She hunched closer in to the fire.

Above, the clear night sky showed vast smears of stars. The bright blue dot of Earth shone brighter than any of them.

"I believe I shall retire for the night," Professor Riemann said, after the dinner was finished. "I am not as young as I once was, and I have important work tomorrow." He rose stiffly, resting his weight on his walking stick. With a brief bow to Mrs. Patterson, he made his way over to his tent.

"We should turn in too, Harry," Bertrand said. "I don't know about you, but I'm completely fagged."

Frustrated, Harriet followed him. She still didn't know, still didn't even have a clue. Every one of the party was suspicious and every one of them was unlikely. Maybe she should have stayed in the Wall after all to look into the maid, Maria, and the Baron de Sorville.

That night, Harriet lay awake long after Bertrand had descended into deep snores in the neighboring tent. The air grew cold in the open clearing as breezes buffeted from the Wall. Harriet was glad she hadn't undressed before climbing into her blankets. The sound of increasingly loud carousing around the fire faded and eventually all she could hear were the sounds of the creatures in the wilderness. It was odd, Harriet thought, as she slowly drifted into sleep. She'd always assumed that the wilderness would be quieter than the city, but it was far more noisy and alive.

Somehow, that felt comforting.

THE EARLY MORNING SUNLIGHT WAS SETTING THE CANVAS aglow when the flap of the tent opened, and Bertrand peered in, yawning. "There you are. I've been sleeping on a stone the size of stegosaurus. Ouch. Any thoughts on how we're going to catch this blasted thief?"

Harriet rolled over, groaning. She hardly felt like she'd fallen asleep and now here was Bertrand waking her up again. Her mouth felt dry and her eyes full of grit.

"Watch them, I suppose." She suppressed a yawn. "See if anyone does anything unusual. The Glass Phantom isn't here for the dinosaur hunt. He was here for the necklace. Maybe he'll give himself away. Now why don't you go and see if there's any breakfast?" She gave him a meaningful look.

Changing her clothes under the blankets wasn't easy in her small tent, but Harriet thanked the heavens she was wearing boys' clothes. If she'd been wearing the kind of dresses Amy always insisted on, she'd have dislocated several limbs. As soon as she was decent, she scrambled out after Bertrand. Most of the party was already up. Matfield and Renton were sitting on a bench, trying to avoid the sunlight and groaning softly to themselves. Major Beaumont was carrying a long gun with a wide barrel cradled in his arms and had already slung a backpack across his shoulders. The rest of the hunters were sitting around the embers of the fire, eating breakfast. Harriet slid in beside Bertrand and took the plate he offered.

Stanley Scott emerged from the large kitchen tent, carrying several guns and a large pack. "We move out in ten minutes!" he called, looking around at the party. "Someone wake Professor Riemann or we'll have to leave him behind."

"I'll do it," Major Beaumont said. "No time for sleeping in!" He made his way over to the professor's tent. "Wake up, Professor!"

There was no answer.

"Cotton wool in his ears I expect," Sir Angus said loudly. "Deuced German. Cotton wool between the ears, too."

Major Beaumont pulled back the flap. "Damn."

"What is it, Major?" Scott called.

"See for yourself." He shook his head. "Damned poor way to start a hunt."

Frowning Harriet hurried over and peeked past the major. "Oh."

The professor was lying in his camp bed, arms crossed carefully across his stomach, his face peaceful, as though sleeping. Be he wasn't sleeping.

"It's the professor," she said, voice trembling. "He's been murdered."

"STAND BACK!" BERTRAND STRODE TOWARD THE TENT. Although his voice was steady, his face looked white.

Harriet was breathing too fast. She could feel her head swimming. She clamped a hand over her mouth to slow her breath. She was *not* going to faint.

A dagger had been driven into the professor's chest, right up to the hilt. His shirt was soaked in blood and the blood had seeped into his bedding. Harriet turned quickly away from the professor's blank, flat eyes. She scrambled past the body to the back of the tent.

The professor's papers lay spread across a portable desk. Harriet saw sketches of dinosaur skeletons surrounded by dozens of annotations in a tiny hand. The professor's walking stick had been knocked over at some point and its chunky, silver dragon-head handle had come loose, but otherwise there was no sign of a struggle. Harriet reached down to pick up the walking stick, and the handle fell off.

"So," Harriet said, turning back to where Bertrand and the major were leaning in through the tent flap and forcing her voice not to shake, "do you want the good news?"

"Good news?" Bertrand whispered. He seemed transfixed by the sight of the professor. Harriet wondered if he'd ever actually seen a dead body before.

"I think you've found the Glass Phantom." She lifted up the dragon-head handle. It was hollow and lined with felt, and inside, Harriet could just make out the glitter of jewels. Carefully, she drew out the countess's stolen necklace.

"Good God." Major Beaumont pushed into the tent. "Never suspected him."

Bertrand shook his head. "This is no good, Harry. I'm supposed to catch him, not let him be murdered in his sleep."

"He wasn't." Major Beaumont leant over the body again. "There's not enough blood."

"There's enough for me," Bertrand said.

"I've seen a lot of men die," the major told him. "His shirt is soaked, but his blankets are hardly wet. He was killed elsewhere and brought back here."

Harriet forced herself to look at the body. It was unnerving how still it was. She'd seen people asleep, and even then there was the slow rise and fall of the chest, the occasional twitch, and unconscious adjustments. She kept expecting this body to move, but it didn't. It just lay there.

She shook herself. She could feel herself panicking. She couldn't let that happen.

She cleared her throat, forcing her mind back to work. "And he's dressed, but not in the same clothes as yesterday. He must have gotten undressed, put on his nightclothes, then gotten dressed again. He must have been going somewhere."

"To meet an accomplice?" the major suggested.

Harriet shook her head. "The Glass Phantom never has accomplices. That's part of why he's been so hard to catch."

Major Beaumont knelt down and reached under the body.

"What are you doing?" Bertrand demanded.

"Turning him over."

"You can't do that!"

"Someone's got to."

With a grunt, the major rolled the body. It flopped loosely over. Harriet had heard that bodies stiffened after death, but the professor's body still seemed limp. *He can't have been dead long.*

"There. See?" The major pointed to the back of the professor's skull. Blood was matted in his thin hair. "Someone struck him from behind. Knocked him out cold, then stabbed him. Probably didn't fancy their chances of overpowering him face-to-face. A coward. If you can't face a man, you shouldn't kill him."

"Maybe you shouldn't kill him at all?" Harriet said, blinking.

The major harrumphed. "Don't always have the choice."

"What I don't understand," Bertrand said, "is why they would bring his body back to the tent if he was killed elsewhere. Why not leave him out there to be eaten by dinosaurs or something? I mean, anyone could have seen them."

Harriet frowned. He was right. It didn't make any sense. The risk was absurd.

"There must have been something about the place he was killed. Some reason they didn't want to risk anyone finding him dead out there. They *want* us to believe he died in the camp."

"What's going on in there?" Stanley Scott demanded, pulling back the tent flap. He stopped, staring down at the body.

"The professor was murdered in the night," Bertrand said. "Someone in this camp killed him."

"Damnation," Scott breathed. "This is not good. Come on then."

"Harry," Bertrand whispered. "How am I supposed to catch a murderer?"

"The same way you'd catch a thief," Harriet said. "Ask questions. Look for clues. Watch people." Not that that had helped them much when they'd been looking for the Glass Phantom. The professor had been a suspect, but no more so than half-a-dozen other members of the party. Asking questions had gotten them nowhere near an answer. "We do have one clue already," she said. "The dagger."

"By Jupiter," the major said. "The young fella has a point. Find the owner of the dagger and you find your murderer."

Bertrand looked back at the body. "Um…"

With a grunt, the major stepped past him, clasped the hilt, and yanked the dagger out of the professor's chest. The sound made Harriet's stomach turn, and she had to look away as the major wiped the dagger clean on the blankets.

They emerged from the tent. The rest of the party had gathered in a somber group by the remains of the bonfire. Bertrand approached them and cleared his throat, straightening his shoulders.

"As you will have overheard, Professor Riemann was murdered last night. I am sorry to have to question you again, but I will need each of you to account for your movements from the time the professor turned in. Perhaps you could start us off, Sir Angus?"

The newspaper proprietor reddened. "You suspect me? *Me?*"

"We don't suspect anyone at the moment," Bertrand said. "We just need to establish the facts."

Sir Angus glared at him. "I retired to my tent soon after you, young man, to work on my memoir. I did not leave it again. And before you ask, no one can confirm that."

"Oh, I think we can," Matfield said with a laugh. "Fellow snored like fire-bull all night. Isn't that right, Renton?"

His friend grunted in agreement and winced. Sir Angus favored them with a glare.

"And how about you two?" Bertrand said.

"I think we were the last ones standing," Matfield said, grinning. "Didn't see anyone after Scott went to bed, and didn't hear anything apart from the fire-bull over there. Sorry, old chap. You're going to have to figure this one out yourself."

Harriet saw a slight look of panic cross her brother-in-law's face. She coughed to draw everyone's attention. "That brings us to you, Mr. Scott."

The guide nodded. "I left the fire at midnight. I did a circuit of the camp, checking the stranglethorn hedges. Everyone was in their tents, other than those two." He indicated Matfield and Renton. "I set out the equipment for the morning, and went to my bed a little before one o'clock. I heard Mr. Matfield and Mr. Renton retire soon after. That was it until dawn."

"Mr. and Mrs. Patterson?" Bertrand asked. "Perhaps you could let us know your movements?"

Mrs. Patterson drew herself up. "I insist that we retire at precisely nine o'clock every night, and I saw no reason to change that. We do not arise until six in the morning."

"And neither of you left the tent for any, ah, personal reason?"

Mrs. Patterson sniffed. "I do not allow such things at night, do I Harold?"

Mr. Patterson's head drooped. "No, dear."

The journalist, Neville Seymour, cleared his throat

awkwardly. "I think I can vouch for Mr. and Mrs. Patterson. My tent is next to theirs and I did not sleep much – the noises of the wilderness, you know – and I am certain neither of them arose."

"And you remained in your tent the whole night?" Bertrand said. "Despite being awake?"

Seymour nodded. "The noises ... unnerved me. I did not wish to go out."

"You may believe him," Mrs. Patterson said. "I pride myself on being a light sleeper. I would have heard him arise, wouldn't I, Harold?"

"As you say, my dear." Mr. Patterson coughed, looking pained. "My wife is ... most attentive."

The major snorted. "Which just leaves me. I slept soundly and I did not awake. A soldier learns to sleep when he can. The noises did not disturb me. I heard and saw nothing."

Harriet sighed. No one had seen anything, and no one had heard anything. Yet the professor had gotten up, and he hadn't been the only one. He'd been killed, then dragged or carried across the camp, all unseen and unheard.

"How about you?" Matfield demanded.

Bertrand started. "I beg your pardon?"

"How do we know it wasn't you?" Matfield said, smirking. "You said you were a policeman, but how do we know that? How do we know you're not the murderer? Sounds like a pretty good cover to me." He looked around the group. "Who's with me?"

Bertrand's cheeks flushed. "I ... ah ..."

Harriet glowered at Matfield and Renton. She was really getting fed up with that pair. She almost hoped they were the murderers just so she could get them locked up.

"Your warrant card," Harriet whispered.

"What? Oh. Yes." With a look of relief, Bertrand pulled the card out of his jacket pocket. The major reached for it

"Looks good to me."

Bertrand took his warrant card back. He was sweating, and Harriet didn't think it was just from the growing heat of the day. Bertrand was out of his depth, and he knew it.

"Ah. Perhaps the dagger?" he said.

The major passed it over, and Bertrand lifted it to where everyone could see. "This is the weapon that killed Professor Riemann. Please take a good look. If any of you have seen it before or know who owns it, please come forward."

There was silence. Mrs. Patterson looked away, her face pale. Bertrand glanced at Harriet, and she shrugged. It had been a long shot.

"Then," Stanley Scott said, "if there are no more questions, I propose that we begin the hunt."

THE MARTIAN WILDERNESS WAS THICK AND DENSE. TALL, twisted trees spiked up through the undergrowth, trailing slowly writhing creepers from their branches.

Beneath the canopy, pressed in by the heavy undergrowth, the air was sweltering. Within ten minutes,
Harriet was soaked through. Sweat dripped from her
forehead into her eyes. She dashed it away with a wet
sleeve.

They were following a narrow animal track. The
undergrowth around them was full of strange rustling
and calls, and the occasional piercing shriek. Harriet
hadn't brought a weapon, but she'd brought several
canisters of dinosaur repellant, and she clutched them
tightly in her damp hands.

Major Beaumont had been as good as his word.
The moment they'd left the camp, he'd struck off on
his own, saying he knew exactly where his Triceratops
watered and he intended to pick up its trail. Nothing
Bertrand could say would dissuade him. Harriet wasn't
sure whether the major should be a suspect. He
certainly had the ability to kill a man, but Harriet
couldn't see any possible motive for him doing so. But
then she couldn't see any motive for anyone, other
than the countess, to kill the professor, and the
countess was two hundred yards up the unclimbable
Wall.

"What are we thinking?" Bertrand said from
behind her, making Harriet jump and almost throw
the canister of repellant at him.

She bit her lip as she steadied herself.
"About what?"

"The murderer, of course! Come on, Harry. I'm
stumped. Most of them seem guilty. Or innocent."

Harriet glanced around. None of the rest of the party were close, but she lowered her voice anyway. "The way I see it, we didn't come across the knife when we searched the luggage and the rest of the party after the countess's jewels were stolen. That leaves two options. Either it was here already, in which case Scott knew about it and he didn't say anything, or it was on one of the people we didn't search: the countess, her maid, or Mrs. Patterson."

The ladies had searched each other in private, but Harriet didn't know how good a job they'd done.

"I think it must have been the maid," Bertrand said. "I never trusted her. She's got a strange nose. I think she must have realized that the professor was the Glass Phantom, so she came down to kill him and retrieve the necklace."

"Except she didn't retrieve it, did she?" Harriet said. "And how would she have gotten down? We'd have heard the airship if it had descended again. It's not exactly quiet."

"That's easy! She left the necklace because she must have known we'd find it and return it to her mistress. And she must have used a hover harness or somesuch."

"But don't you think we would have seen a hover harness when we were searching? She could hardly have hidden that under her petticoats."

Bertrand shook his head. "I tell you, it's her. Or maybe that journalist. He didn't have an alibi."

Nor a reason, Harriet thought. Which was more the

pity, because if he were the murderer, she'd have a free run at the newspaper article.

The path dipped down to a shallow creek before crossing and climbing a high bank. Crab-fish scuttled away from their feet as they splashed across. The water felt wonderfully cool against Harriet's feet. She paused for a minute, peering up the stream, where the stalking-grass and twitch-bushes arched over the water, dipping long roots in to drink.

She blinked to clear the sweat from her eyes again, and in that moment, she thought she saw a face staring back at her from the undergrowth further up the stream.

"Look!" she hissed to Bertrand.

He splashed over to her. "What?"

She peered closer, but the face was gone. "Up there," she said. "I saw someone. I think it was the major."

Bertrand cupped his hands around his mouth. "Hey!" he shouted. "Come out!"

The undergrowth shook. A small dinosaur with a low, mottled body, long tail, and a small head burst out and darted away up the stream.

"There you are!" Bertrand said, grinning. "You spooked it. Mind you, those jowls did look a bit like the major."

Harriet let out a sigh. She'd been so sure. But she couldn't stop her heart fluttering. She'd seen a dinosaur! A real one! She'd seen pictures, of course, but somehow she'd never imagined them looking so *real* in the flesh.

"Up here!" a voice called from further up the animal path.

Bertrand met Harriet's eyes and shrugged. "Let's see what they want."

The rest of the party members were crouching below the ridgeline a hundred yards up the path. Scott motioned them down as they approached.

"The pack of Coelophysis are on the other side of the ridge," Scott said. "They're feeding, but they'll detect us as soon as we cross. They have excellent vision, and they are fast, agile, and intelligent. They wouldn't normally hunt humans, but they might attack if they feel threatened, and they *will* defend their kill. Spread out in pairs and approach quietly. Do not discharge your weapons until you can see your target. Clear? Good. Let's go."

"Well, Harry?" Bertrand said, drawing her away from the others. "What do you say?"

"I'm not killing them!" Dinosaurs were a rarity, confined by the Great Wall to this single peninsula, no larger than France on Earth. She couldn't imagine why anyone would want to reduce their numbers any further.

"I know. But don't you want a better look? We only caught a glimpse of that one by the stream. How many people can say they've seen a dinosaur close up?"

It would be something, Harriet thought. And it would add color to her story when she wrote it up. The

more color the better when she had to compete with
Neville Seymour. She could already see Neville
creeping his way up the ridge in Sir Angus's bullish
wake. Anyway, they were hardly like to pick up any
clues in the middle of the hunt. What harm could
it do?

"Come on, then!" Bertrand said. He was grinning
like a loon for almost the first time since he'd taken on
the task of tracking down the Glass Phantom. He cut
off to the side and ducked his way into the undergrowth. Harriet followed. Sleeve-creepers tried to wrap
themselves around her arms, their flowers turning in
like suction cups to fix on her skin, but she shook
them off.

Together, they pushed the branches of a deluge-
bush aside, ignoring the sticky sap sprinkling down
around them, and peered over the ridge.

In the center of a clearing two hundred yards away,
a dozen small dinosaurs were clustered around a
carcass. Each creature stood waist-high on two sturdy
back legs. They had long, slim heads and feathery
hairs jutting back from their long necks and shoulders.
Their skin was an orangey-brown with short black
stripes. Their underbellies were creamy white. Sharp,
serrated teeth cut and tore at the flesh of whatever prey
they had taken down. Every few seconds, one or
another of them would startle upright, its head
twitching around, large, yellow eyes scanning the
undergrowth.

"Bit closer?" Bertrand whispered.

Harriet nodded, her pulse pounding in her ears. Slowly, so as not to disturb the bushes around them, she slithered forward. Small stones jabbed into her belly and chest, but she ignored them.

A sudden shot sounded, cracking through the air. In less than a second, the pack of Coelophysis had scattered, like fish in a stream under a footfall. Harriet peered around, but she couldn't see any of the other hunters.

"Damn them," Bertrand muttered. "Where have the creatures gone?"

The Coelophysis had disappeared like shadows. Harriet felt the sweat turn suddenly cold on her skin.

"Do you think they've fled?" she said.

Bertrand stood, his hand resting on his belt of stunstars. "Scott said they'd defend their kill." The carcass was still lying in the middle of the clearing. "Whatever we do, we mustn't make them think we're after it. Let's move back. Carefully."

Gritting her teeth, Harriet retreated, one step at a time. She clutched a canister of dinosaur repellant, ready to pull the seal and send it spinning toward the Coelophysis. She couldn't see them anywhere.

A loud shout sounded to their right, then a flurry of shots, followed by a whoop. "Almost got one!" one of the young men yelled. Harriet heard crashing in the undergrowth as whoever it was pursued his prey.

"Idiots," Harriet muttered. Her breath sounded too loud in her ears. The forest had gone silent, save for the blundering of the hunters, and the occasional, whispering rush of some creature racing for cover. Harriet's fingers were so tight on her canister, she wondered if she'd be able to actually let it go if she needed to throw it.

A stick cracked to her left, and she spun, her hand coming around, before she saw Bertrand standing with one foot off the ground.

"Sorry," he mouthed.

"We need to find some clear space," Harriet said. "Somewhere we can see what's coming." The undergrowth here was so thick, she could scarcely see five yards in any direction.

Bertrand nodded. "This way. I think." He pushed a bush carefully aside and stepped past, holding the branches for Harriet.

The undergrowth in front of them shivered. Harriet tensed. Every breath felt tight in her chest. It was as though someone was holding a pillow over her face, forcing her to fight to suck in air. She knew her eyes must be bulging.

A screech sounded, not a dozen yards ahead, and Harriet saw a flash of orange and white dart toward them.

Bertrand spun, grabbing her arm. "This way!"

"No." Harriet planted her feet. She was close to panic, but she hadn't lost her senses yet. "They're pack hunters. It's trying to drive us. Come on!"

She sprinted toward where she'd glimpsed the Coelophysis, throwing her canister ahead of her. It exploded, spraying liquid around it. The stench acrid chemicals burned at her nose and made her eyes water. The Coelophysis shrieked. Harriet kept on running. She felt Bertrand's footsteps behind her. More shrieks sounded further back.

They burst into a clearing around a tall ice-bark tree. Its smooth trunk glinted in the sunlight. Harriet put her back to it, pulling out another canister. A moment later, Bertrand joined her.

"How did you know?" he panted, looking around, wild-eyed.

"Scott said they're intelligent pack hunters. Pack hunters often use one of their number to drive their prey toward the main pack."

Bertrand nodded, dropping his hands onto his knees. "Doesn't look like they followed. I think we're safe for—"

The crystalline bark of the tree exploded above his head, sending shards spinning above them like thrown razors.

"Down!" Bertrand grabbed her and threw her to the ground. She hit with enough force to knock the breath from her chest. She blinked tears from her eyes as she gasped for air. Bertrand had pulled a stun-star and set its clockwork motor whirring. He scanned the undergrowth, ready to throw it. "Someone shot at us!"

A moment later, Stanley Scott burst into the clearing. "Are you all right? I heard the pack and I heard a shot."

"Did you shoot at us?" Harriet demanded.

Scott shook his head. "Not me." He lifted his gun.

"Still loaded, see?" He scanned the undergrowth. All was quiet.

Slowly, Bertrand let Harriet rise. "I think we're safe now."

Scott produced a hand siren from his backpack and wound it. The high rising and falling tone cut through the noises of the wilderness. A minute later, Matfield and Renton appeared from the undergrowth, grinning, guns slung over their shoulders. Bertrand drew Harriet to one side.

"That shot was on purpose," he hissed.

Harriet stared at him. "Are you sure?"

He nodded. "Someone tried to kill us! Why would anyone want to kill us?"

Harriet's forehead furrowed. "They must think you're on to them for the professor's murder."

"But I'm not onto anyone!"

Which was true. They didn't even have a prime suspect yet. So why would someone think they had?

"It would help if we knew *why* Professor Riemann was murdered," Harriet said. "It can't have been for the necklace, or it would have been taken. Maybe he saw something he shouldn't have or someone had a grudge against him."

Could he really have offended someone so badly? He hadn't acted like he'd known any of the other passengers. Or had someone known he was the Glass Phantom and come looking for revenge over something? She shook her head. There was no point speculating. They needed evidence. Clues. Answers. Not guesses.

Bertrand looked worried. "That means there's something else going on that we don't know about. Harry, it was hard enough to find the Glass Phantom when we knew what he was up to. How are we supposed to capture someone when we don't have a clue what's going on?"

The last of the hunters to appear were the Pattersons. They emerged from the undergrowth, Mr. Patterson looking red in the face. He'd received some kind of insect bite on the tip of his nose, and it had swollen horribly. Mrs. Patterson looked disgusted as she followed her husband out.

"Harold thought he saw a Tyrannosaurus rex. Just managed to shoot a bush." She glared at him. "Mr. and Mrs. Casson will be *unbearable* if you come home without a proper head."

"Ladies and gentlemen," Scott called. "As you have seen, hunting dinosaurs is not as easy as you might have thought. There is a small lake a mile or so from here where dinosaurs often come to drink. There is a good chance that you will be able to get close enough to shoot some specimens."

Or for someone to shoot us, Harriet thought. This time, she wouldn't let the rest of the party out of her sight.

∼

It was growing dark by the time they made it back to base camp, and the sun was casting long shadows across the face of the Great Wall. Sir Angus had brought down an immature stegosaurus, while Matfield and Renton had spent the afternoon taking shots at a herd of Dryosauruses every time they came down to the water. Mr. Patterson had failed to hit anything with his compressed-air rifle, and his wife was glaring at him in tight-lipped silence. Harriet had spent the day watching the rest of the party carefully, but no one had acted suspiciously, and by the time they reached the camp she was seething in frustration.

"Tomorrow," Scott told them, after dinner was finished and the fire was dying down, "we will track down some larger prey. If any of you have had enough of the hunt, you may join Lady Krakendorff and her companions at the viewing lodge on Elliot's Hill. Either way, we'll be starting early. Get some sleep."

Sleep sounded wonderful. Harriet was aching all over and she felt filthy. Long days confined in Amy's drawing room sewing and reading or taking gentle strolls around the Tharsis City parks hadn't prepared her for this amount of exertion.

There were two wash-tents in the camp, one for the men and one for the ladies. For the first time, Harriet regretted dressing as a boy for the expedition. She barely had time to run a wet cloth over her face and neck before she heard Matfield and Renton heading for the wash-tent and had to flee. Maybe she'd be able to wipe herself down in her tent, but it was hardly a substitute for a proper bath.

Fighting the urge to scratch her skin where the dried sweat had left her itchy and irritable, she made her way with Bertrand back to their tents.

"I've been thinking about this all day," she said, "and I'm sure I was right. Professor Riemann saw something he shouldn't. After he stole the necklace, he must have been on the lookout in case anyone suspected he was the Glass Phantom. He must have spotted someone behaving strangely. Whatever they were up to, it was enough to get him killed."

Bertrand leaned against his tent pole, sagging. "But what were they doing?"

Harriet shrugged. "The only way we're going to find that out is if we catch them at it, too. There's a good chance that Professor Riemann interrupted whatever they were up to. They may try again tonight."

The camp settled more quickly than it had the previous night, and Harriet lay there in the dark, listening to the sounds of the Martian wilderness and the heavy movements of enormous beasts just beyond the stranglethorn hedge. She still had no idea who might be behind the professor's murder, and she lay there, skin prickling in frustration. If Bertrand couldn't solve the murder, then the recovery of the countess's necklace would count for nothing. Bertrand would still lose his job and she wouldn't have a satisfactory story to sell. She would have to marry some idiotic young man and keep house for him. She couldn't bear it.

Thick clouds were closing in across the stars. Far away, Harriet heard the rumble of thunder. She'd kept the flap of her tent open, so she could watch the camp, and now swirling wind bullied its way in, snatching at her blankets and carrying with it the thick humidity of the forest.

The day had been long and difficult, and her body was exhausted. She pinched herself to keep awake. Over in the next tent, she heard Bertrand's faint snores. If she was wrong about this and nothing happened, she'd regret it tomorrow.

Lightning flickered above the trees and whip-vines lashed uneasily above the canopy. Raindrops pattered like small stones on the canvas of her tent. Harriet shivered and pulled the tent flap tightly closed, leaving only a small slit for her to peer out. As if it had only been waiting for her action, the rain swept across the trees with a rush and hit the camp, extinguishing the last of the fire's coals. It sounded like a waterfall pounding onto the canvas. All the sounds of the wilderness disappeared under the onslaught. Harriet could scarcely see a dozen yards from her tent. She shaded her eyes and waited.

Another yawn forced itself out. She didn't know if she was going to make this. Then she saw them: two shapes, hunched beneath thick cloaks, crossing the camp. In the downpour she couldn't make out who they were, but why would anyone be out in this if they didn't have to be? She watched them for a moment. They were heading for the hedge, not for one of the tents. The professor must have seen the same thing last night.

And he was killed, she reminded herself. Well, she would be more careful. She *had* to find out who had killed him. Pulling on her waterproof cloak, Harriet slipped out of her tent and across to Bertrand's. She shook him awake.

"They're on the move," she whispered.

"What?" Bertrand blinked up at her. "Who are?"

"The murderers. Come *on!*"

"But it's raining."

Harriet shook her head and peered out the tent. The figures she'd seen had disappeared in the downpour.

"We're losing them."

Grumbling, Bertrand hauled himself up, and Harriet led him in the direction the cloaked figures had gone. There was no sign of them, but the narrow gap they'd opened in the stranglethorn hedge was still closing slowly. Harriet stroked the hedge apart, and she and Bertrand hurried in pursuit.

Beyond the hedge, the wilderness began in earnest. Thick trees dripped relentlessly into the deep shadows, and crawlspines, brought out by the rain, crept across the narrow path. Harriet stepped carefully around them to avoid the spines they shot out at anything that moved nearby.

"Any idea who we're following?" Bertrand asked. The rain was beginning to ease at last, although a steady sheet of water still sluiced down the side of the

Great Wall to their right, running away in dozens of small streams.

"Just that there are two of them."

As the rain faded to a thin drizzle and the humidity rose again, the sounds of the wilderness returned. Creatures shrieked and howled in the high branches. In the distance, a slow, deep trumpeting rolled across the trees. Bushes shook and twigs cracked. Unseen things flapped suddenly away. Despite the lingering heat, Harriet found herself shivering and glancing nervously around at every sound. What had seemed exotic and exciting in the day was terrifying in the dark.

The underbrush crunched loudly off to their left. Harriet froze, her hand resting on Bertrand's arm. That had been close. Really close. Slowly, she turned her head. Trees shook and drops of water pattered down onto wide leaves. The wilderness, Harriet noticed, had suddenly turned silent. Even the crawlspines had stopped, hunching into little prickly balls.

"We have to get off the path," Harriet whispered.

Still watching the trees, they eased themselves back into the cover of a thick clusterball bush. Harriet sank down into the puddled rain, feeling cold water seep through her jacket, waistcoat, and shirt.

A loud snuffling followed by a low rumble shivered the canopy. A heavy footstep shook the ground, followed by another. Branches splintered. Then, as the rainclouds parted to let through thin starlight, a vast creature appeared. The dinosaur was three or four times Bertrand's height. It walked on two powerful legs, holding its massive tail well above the ground. A head as long as Harriet's body turned slowly, surveying the undergrowth. Long teeth showed as the dinosaur growled softly. Harriet could smell the stink of rotting meat.

"A Tyrannosaurus rex," Bertrand breathed.

Harriet hunched down further, her hand resting on a canister of dinosaur repellant. *Would it work on a Tyrannosaurus rex?* She hoped she'd never get a chance to find out. She fought the urge to fidget and wondered just how fast a T. rex could run.

Then it caught a scent. Its head turned, and it lumbered off back into the trees. At last the sound of breaking branches faded and was gone.

Bertrand let out a shaky laugh. "I can't believe anyone would want to *hunt* something like that."

Noises started to return to the wilderness, the calls of small animals and rustling, scurrying sounds of creatures in the undergrowth. Something called in a sharp, high voice from high up in the trees. On the path, the crawlspines unfurled.

"Come on," Harriet said. "We're going to lose them."

Bertrand laid a hand on her back. "Don't!"

"What?"

"Look. There." Bertrand indicated a spot just under Harriet's arm. Carefully, she twisted her head around. A line of tiny beetles was emerging from a hole in a rotten branch directly beneath her.

"Those are weaver beetles. You know. The professor told us about them. The Artherton expedition? They're what turned Artherton and Connolly's bodies to crystal."

Harriet stared down at the line of beetles and gritted her teeth. They looked so tiny and innocent, but if she shifted a single inch they would be crawling up inside her jacket. Her muscles tensed tighter than a steel-vine. Her teeth felt like they were going to crack from her clenched jaw. Did weaver beetles only colonize dead bodies, or did they kill their hosts?

Every moment, their suspects were getting further and further away, but the beetles just kept on coming. Harriet wanted to scream in frustration, but she didn't dare open her mouth.

"All right," Bertrand breathed at last. "I think they've gone."

Harriet let out a breath. Her body trembled from the released tension.

"Think we've lost our quarries?" Bertrand asked.

Harriet pushed herself to her feet, tried to brush the mud and water from the front of her outfit, then gave up.

"I don't know. We could go back to the camp and see who's missing. Find out who they were."

Bertrand shook his head. "That's no good. We have to catch them doing something. Otherwise they're just a couple of people taking a stroll."

"In the pouring rain, out among the dinosaurs."

But Bertrand was right. With no idea what the pair were up to, she and Bertrand would have nothing.

The path continued on for at least a mile, meandering at times around stands of serpent oaks, before dipping into a shallow valley that abutted the Great Wall. Two figures stood in a small clearing at the base of the Wall, still hooded and cloaked. Bertrand pulled Harriet from the path, and they sank down in the undergrowth, watching.

"What do you think they're up to?" Harriet whispered. As far as she could see, the two figures were just standing at the bottom of the Great Wall, staring up into the blackness. A moment later, the shorter of the two figures reached under his cloak and produced a friction lamp, similar to the ones Harriet had seen in the passageways of the Great Wall. Sheltering it with his cloak, the figure flashed the lamp several times up the side of the Wall. A moment later, a whirring sound began high up above them.

Frowning, Harriet peered upward. Although the storm clouds were clearing and Mars's two small moons were high above the horizon, the vast black bulk of the Wall made it hard to see anything.

The whirring grew louder as Harriet and Bertrand crouched there.

"This is odd, Harry," Bertrand said. "Don't you think this is odd?"

It certainly didn't seem like something worth killing over. It was just ... odd.

Finally, Harriet spotted something slowly

descending toward the two waiting figures. It was a cylindrical object half the size of a man, and dangling from it was what looked like a small package. It was floating down as lightly as a feather from one of the storm hawks.

When it reached the ground, the two figures hurried forward, unhooked the package, and the cylinder began to rise again.

"Now what are they doing?" Harriet asked.

Bertrand frowned. "Someone's dropping them something down from the Wall. But we're nowhere near the docking bay."

Which meant that whatever was coming down wasn't coming from anyone in their party. "Remember what Professor Riemann said? There are teams of archaeologists working in the Wall. Someone in one those teams must be dropping something."

Bertrand shook his head. "But why? Why go to all that effort? And why *kill* someone over it?"

Harriet's mind was racing now. "The professor said that there were still Ancient Martian artifacts in the Wall. Every great invention in the last hundred years has been built on what we've learned from Ancient Martian artifacts. No one's uncovered a new dragon tomb for almost ten years, but they're still finding stuff here. Imagine if you could get your hands on something that no one else knew about? Some completely new technology? Imagine how much money you could make!" She met her brother-in-law's eyes. "They're smuggling artifacts from the Wall. Riemann saw them do it, they killed him to keep him quiet, then they moved his body so no one would discover their drop site."

"And now we've seen them," Bertrand said.

The words made Harriet feel uneasy. She glanced across at the figures, but they were peering back up the Wall again.

"We have to arrest them," Bertrand said, grimly. "Not just for smuggling but for murder, too."

Harriet shivered. She tried to tell herself it was from the rain. "What if they're armed?"

Bertrand straightened. "I don't have a choice, Harry. I'm a policeman. This is my job." He glanced at her. "You should stay under cover."

Harriet shook her head. "No." There was no way she was letting her brother-in-law go in there alone.

Bertrand nodded and passed her a stun-star. "You know how to use this?"

"Yes." Her lips felt dry. She worked her mouth to moisten them.

"Then we go in fast, before they can reach their weapons. Don't hesitate to use your stun-star."

Carefully, they crept down the animal track, approaching the two figures. Harriet still couldn't make out who they were. Her hand clutching the stun-star felt sweaty and slippery, and she had to blink to keep her eyes clear. Bertrand looked hardly less nervous. All it would take would be for one of the figures to turn at the wrong time. They crept closer.

They were still forty yards away when the taller figure straightened suddenly and spun.

"Hold still!" Bertrand barked. "You're under arrest. If you go for your weapons, I *will* fire."

The figures froze.

"Take down your hoods," Bertrand ordered. "Now."

Harriet flicked the switch on her stun-star. Its clockwork motor began to spin. She lifted it.

Slowly, reluctantly, the two figures pulled their hoods down. Mr. and Mrs. Patterson stood looking back at them. Harriet blinked.

"You are under arrest for smuggling and for the murder of Professor Riemann," Bertrand said. "We will take you into custody, and you will pay for your crimes back in Tharsis City."

"I am very sorry," a voice said from behind them. "But I really cannot allow you to do that."

HARRIET TURNED, HER STUN-STAR RAISED. NEVILLE Seymour was standing behind them, a gun pointed directly at Harriet. His face looked white and his hands were trembling, but even from that distance, there was no way he could miss.

"Drop your weapons," he said. "Please. I'd really rather not hurt you."

Grimacing, Harriet flicked off the stun-star and let it fall. *Why hadn't they looked behind them?* They'd been stupid to assume the Pattersons were on their own.

Was this what had happened to the professor? Neville had snuck up on him while he was watching and then what? Had he surrendered and been killed? Or had he tried to resist?

"Good." Neville glanced over to the Pattersons. "You're not going to...?" He trailed off.

"They've seen our faces," Mrs. Patterson said. "We can't let them go free."

If anything, Neville looked whiter than ever. "Couldn't we just ... leave them here? Tied up or something?"

Mr. Patterson bent over and picked up his gun. "You're an idiot, Seymour. Just don't forget you've got as much to lose as we do if they live."

Harriet watched them carefully. Neville still had his gun trained on her, but his hands were shaking.

A whirring noise came from above them. Harriet glanced up to see the cylinder descending the Great Wall again, bringing another package down. The sound of the cylinder's propeller was loud against the silence of the night.

It took Harriet a moment to realize what she was hearing. Or, more to the point, what she wasn't hearing.

The wilderness had gone silent. Again. Nothing was moving. Nothing was calling.

The hairs on her arms and neck stood painfully erect.

Harriet closed her eyes, said a quick prayer, then tipped back her head and shouted, "Over here!"

Mr. Patterson swung toward them, his face creasing in fury.

The T. rex burst from the undergrowth like a steam bull. Branches shattered and spun through the air. The ground shook. Harriet stumbled back at its ferocity. The beast was only twenty yards away, to their left, and it towered over them. Its jaws looked wide enough to swallow her whole.

Neville shrieked, and Harriet saw his gun waver. She swung her arm, knocking the gun aside. Neville's finger twitched violently on the trigger.

The bullet snatched past Harriet. She heard a buzz like a bore-beetle and felt wind on her cheek. She grabbed Bertrand and ran. From the foot of the Wall, Mr. Patterson fired at them, but the bullet went wide.

"Where are we going?" Bertrand demanded. Harriet was leading them on an arc away from the T. rex and toward the Wall, near where the Pattersons were standing. On either side, high trees and thick undergrowth grew right up to the smooth rock. There was no way out.

Behind them, the Tyrannosaurus rex bellowed. Its voice shivered the damp air. It pounded after them.

"The T. rex, you fool!" Mrs. Patterson screamed at her husband. "Shoot the T. rex!"

Mr. Patterson ejected the spent compressed-air cartridge and slammed in a fresh one. He scrambled desperately to reset the valves.

Harriet ducked to the side, pulling Bertrand after her. Clutch-vines snapped at them from the undergrowth. Harriet kicked her foot free and kept on running. Mr. Patterson dropped to one knee, sighting along his barrel.

"Shoot!" Mrs. Patterson shouted.

Grimacing, Mr. Patterson pulled the trigger. Harriet heard the pop of expelled air followed by a dull thud.

The T. rex roared in fury. Harriet risked a glance back. She could see where the bullet had hit the creature, high up on its chest, near its right shoulder, and she could see the trail of blood, but all it seemed to have done was enrage the dinosaur. With a shake of its head, it broke into a run.

Neville had finally shaken off his paralysis and was sprinting after them, but the Tyrannosaurus rex was gaining on him with every step. Harriet gritted her teeth and ran harder. Her breath burned in her chest and her throat felt raw, like she was dragging sandpaper back and forth inside it.

Mr. Patterson fumbled a compressed air cylinder and dropped it. It bounced away from him, over the red stones. He scrambled after it.

"What are we going to do?" Bertrand panted.

Harriet didn't waste breath answering. She just put her head down and kept running. They *had* to reach the Wall before the dinosaur.

Mrs. Patterson shoved her husband to one side, wrenching the gun from him. "Give it to me, you idiot!" With a single, smooth movement, she pushed in the cylinder and twisted the valves. She stalked past her husband, advancing on the T. rex, eyes tight. Then

Harriet and Bertrand were past the pair of them, and the Wall loomed up above them, vast and high and dark. Its surface was smooth and impossible to climb.

Mrs. Patterson stood in front of the T. rex as it charged. She lifted the gun, sighted, and fired. The bullet caught the T. rex on the snout. Its massive head whipped back in pain. Then it lunged.

Mrs. Patterson didn't even have time to take a step back. The T. rex's jaws snapped closed around her, below the waist. For a second, Harriet saw her legs kicking wildly, then a cloud covered the moons, and the view was dimmed.

Bertrand gasped beside her. Harriet shook her head. She couldn't afford to think about what the creature had just done to Mrs. Patterson. She stumbled up to the Great Wall. Its smooth stone felt cold under her palms.

"There's no way up." Bertrand pressed his back to the Wall, watching the T. rex.

The lifting cylinder was still hovering just above the ground to their right. A small, heavy sack dangled from it. Harriet unhooked it and let it fall with a metallic *clank* to the ground.

"Grab hold of this," she said, hauling the cylinder across to Bertrand. It was the size of his torso, and she could feel the whirr of the propeller inside.

The T. rex had finished with the remains of Mrs. Patterson and now it stalked toward them. Mr. Patterson backed away from it, hands clenching and unclenching, his shoulders stiff with fear.

Bertrand grabbed a handle on the side of the cylinder.

"Tight," Harriet said. Then she reached up, turned the lifting dial to full, and clung on to a second handle.

The powerful springs inside the lifting cylinder began to unwind. Air blasted downward, feeling like a hurricane battering against Harriet's legs. The cylinder shot upward, wrenching Harriet's arms. Her wet hands slipped. She gripped tighter as her feet left the ground.

Neville threw himself forward, catching hold of the cylinder. It swung wildly, yanking them to the side, away from the Wall, then back. They hit the Wall hard. The blow sent stars cascading across Harriet's vision. The cylinder stabilized itself and they were rising again. The ground looked far below, even though her feet were scarcely head-high above the ground.

With a roar, the Tyrannosaurus rex broke into a run. Mr. Patterson screamed, turned on his heels and fled. He threw himself up, grabbing hold of Neville's legs and sending the cylinder swaying again. Neville tried to kick his legs free. The propeller whined, its sound rising desperately.

"We're too heavy!" Bertrand said.

The cylinder was rising, but too slowly. The Tyrannosaurus rex lumbered toward them. They rose to the level of its head, and Harriet saw raw meat still caught on its long, yellow teeth, and a torn strip of Mrs. Patterson's dress.

The Tyrannosaurus rex lunged. Harriet swung up her legs and kicked off against the Wall. The cylinder wobbled outward, away from the T. rex's scything jaws. Then they were out of reach.

"How much power does this thing have?" Bertrand choked out. Harriet could already hear how much the cylinder was straining. It couldn't have been designed to lift four fully-grown people.

"Not enough," she managed.

"I don't think we're lifting anymore," Neville said.

Harriet glanced down and immediately wished she hadn't. They hung thirty or forty feet above the T. rex, but it hadn't moved and they weren't getting any higher. It was watching them with small eyes.

"They hunt by scent, don't they?" Bertrand said.

Harriet nodded. And the lifter was blasting their scent right down at the T. rex.

The sound of the propeller fell in pitch. The lifter cylinder dropped an arm's length, then stabilized. The jolt sent pain shooting through Harriet's shoulders.

"We're going to go down," she said.

Mr. Patterson let go of Neville's legs with one hand and grabbed at Harriet. She kicked his hand away.

"Can you reach your dinosaur repellant?" Bertrand called over the sound of the laboring propeller. He had hooked one arm through his handle and pulled out a stun-star with his free hand.

"You're not going to knock out a dinosaur with that!" Mr. Patterson shrieked.

"Shut up!" Harriet snapped. She pulled herself up, ignoring the way the cylinder swayed and dropped again. Hooking her arm through the metal handle was agonizing. It bit into the crook of her arm as if it were pulling her elbow apart. Grimacing, she reached down to the dinosaur repellent at her belt. She had four canisters left.

"Drop them all," Bertrand said.

Harriet took a steadying breath. She had no idea if the repellant would be enough to drive away the T. rex, but she did know she couldn't afford to waste any. She unclipped the canister, pulled the seal, and let it drop. It hit the T. rex full on the snout. The creature reared back, its head shaking back and forth to rid it of the stink. Harriet dropped the second, then the third and the fourth. Liquid spattered from the cylinders, engulfing the Tyrannosaurus rex's muzzle and dripping onto its flanks. It bellowed in fury, its enormous mouth snapping wildly, spittle spraying around. Then it retreated, still tossing its head furiously.

The lifter fell. The propeller screamed in protest, desperately beating the air, but the power was failing. They plunged toward the ground. At the last moment, Harriet let go, throwing herself to the side. She'd meant to roll, but she didn't have the time or the control. She landed on her back in a small bush. Twigs and branches scratched her arms, legs, and back and tangled in her hair. She tore herself free just in time to see Bertrand stagger to his feet.

The Tyrannosaurus rex had retreated, but it hadn't fled altogether. It paced heavily twenty feet away, shaking its enormous head, its eyes never leaving them. Harriet wondered how long the repellant would last.

Bertrand flicked the switch on his stun-star. The clockwork motor spun, and Bertrand threw it as though he were skimming a stone. It arced across the clearing to bury one of its spikes into the T. rex's hide. The impact wasn't enough to hurt the gigantic dinosaur, but the moment it was fixed into the hide, it released an electrostatic charge that was enough to knock a man unconscious. The T. rex flinched back as though it had been bitten. Its head came down, looking for its attacker, and Bertrand sent a second stun-star skimming into the dinosaur. The creature twisted, snapping at the air.

Bertrand met Harriet's eyes. "Last one," he said, and threw the final stun-star.

The stun-star thudded into the T. rex's jaw. Its head jerked back involuntarily. Its body shuddered. Its eyes turned on Bertrand. Teeth glistened in the starlight.

Harriet's hands clenched into fists. This was it. They had no more ideas and no more weapons.

Then the T. rex turned and lumbered away. At last, the sounds of the wilderness returned.

Harriet pulled herself from the bush and hurried across to her brother-in-law. "Are you all right?"

Bertrand grimaced. "Hurt my knee in the fall. I'll survive. Not going to be running any races for a while, though."

Mr. Patterson and Neville untangled themselves

from where they had fallen. Neville was bleeding from a cut on his forehead.

"Harold Patterson and Neville Seymour," Bertrand said, limping painfully toward them. "You are under arrest for the murder of Professor Riemann. I am taking you into custody and back to Tharsis City, where you will stand trial for your crimes."

Mr. Patterson's eyes narrowed. He reached behind him and pulled out a long, sharp knife.

"And how, exactly," he said, "do you plan to do that, when you will not leave this clearing alive?"

HARRIET GLANCED DESPERATELY AROUND. MR. Patterson wasn't a big man, but with that knife he didn't have to be. Bertrand had been trained in unarmed combat when he'd joined the police service, but Harriet knew her brother-in-law had never been good at it. The best advice he'd been able to give her was to run, but he wasn't going to run anywhere with that injured knee.

"You killed my wife," Mr. Patterson shouted, stalking toward them. "You've ruined *everything*! You'll never arrest me!"

"They won't have to." A bulky figure stepped out of the trees. He was carrying a large gun and it was aimed directly at Mr. Patterson.

"Major Beaumont?" Bertrand said, jaw dropping.

"Please drop your weapon, Mr. Patterson, and step away from it."

The little man glared at the major, his eyes full of fury.

"Please do not imagine that I will not shoot you, Mr. Patterson. I have shot men before."

"What are you doing?" Bertrand demanded.

"I am arresting them for you," the major said. His heavy jowls twitched in a smile. "I am afraid I have misled you all somewhat. I did not come here to hunt dinosaurs. I work for the British-Martian Intelligence Service, and I have been tracking a gang of artifact smugglers for five years. I have never been able to find out how they have been getting artifacts from the Wall, but it seems you have been able to do that for me. Your knife, Mr. Patterson," he added, gesturing with the gun.

With a glare, Mr. Patterson dropped his knife and stepped away from it.

"If you would do me the favor, Mr. Simpson? I believe you are carrying rope?"

Bertrand nodded. He crossed to Mr. Patterson and quickly tied the smuggler's hands behind his back, before moving on to do the same for Neville. The young journalist's head hung low, and he didn't look up to meet anyone's eyes.

"I didn't want anyone to get hurt," the journalist whispered. "I had debts. Bad debts..."

"And you will be questioned thoroughly back in Tharsis City," the major said brusquely. "Save your excuses until then." He turned to Harriet. "I must congratulate you, Miss George. In a couple of days, you did what I could not in five years. You caught the smugglers in the act. I am very impressed."

"Miss George?" Mr. Patterson demanded. "What's he talking about?"

Harriet felt her cheeks color. "You saw through my disguise?"

"A necessity in my line of work." The major stepped close to her and dropped his voice. "A line of work for which you have shown a remarkable aptitude."

Harriet frowned. "What do you mean?"

"Mr. Patterson and our young friend there are not the ringleaders of this gang. The same gang members have never been sent here twice. I do not know how they recruit, because I have not been able to establish connections between any of the passengers who have been on each of the expeditions. We may have stopped this particular operation, but whoever is behind it is still out there, and they have been selling the artifacts to enemies of British Mars. I know for a fact that several dangerous artifacts have been sold to agents of Napoleon Bonaparte. I must find whoever is behind this or they will locate another supply of artifacts, and we will have achieved nothing here. I think you might be of great help."

Harriet peered at him. "Help? How?"

"I believe you are to enter Society within two years."

Harriet's jaw dropped. "How do you know that?"

"I have extensive information on each member of this expedition. I believe that whoever is behind this gang is a member of good Society in Tharsis City, or at least visits it regularly. A man like me will get nowhere in Society, but I think you might. If you were willing to, I would like to ask you to join the Intelligence Service and attempt to track down the ringleader." He raised his eyebrows. "Unless you have your heart set on a quiet marriage, that is?"

THEY ARRIVED BACK IN THARSIS CITY A WEEK LATER, as the last streams of the shimmer-stream pollen migration drifted away from the flanks of the extinct volcano.

Harriet wasn't sure that she'd actually *missed* the city, but there had been one thing she'd been looking forward to all the way back: the look on the faces of the Police Commissioner and the other Inspectors of the Tharsis City Police Service when Bertrand brought in not only the body of the Glass Phantom, but also the recovered jewels *and* the thief's murderers. It might have been a little petty, but she could scarcely suppress her grin as they gaped at Bertrand when he led Mr. Patterson and Neville into the police headquarters.

The story of the expedition, written by an anonymous, previously unpublished correspondent and printed by Sir Angus Cameron in *The Tharsis Times*, meant that there was absolutely no chance that

Bertrand could be sacked. In a thundering leader column, Sir Angus demanded to know why the heroic gentleman who had caught the Glass Phantom was still only a lowly Inspector. Harriet was certain a promotion would be coming in the very near future.

As Harriet shook hands with the other passengers alighting from the airship, Major Beaumont leaned in close and whispered, "A message will arrive at your house tomorrow morning inviting you to tea at a young lady's house. You will accept and present yourself to the address provided at eleven o'clock sharp. Your training for the British-Martian Intelligence Service will be vigorous, harsh, and demanding." He met her eyes. "I do not anticipate that you will encounter many problems with it."

Then he nodded, and disappeared into the crowds.

Harriet let out a satisfied sigh. Life was about to get very, very interesting at last.

- The End -

If you enjoyed The Dinosaur Hunters, please consider leaving a review at Goodreads or one of your other favorite books websites. It really does help get the word out.

You can also sign up to my newsletter via my website (patricksamphire.com) so that you'll be the first to find out about new books and stories, as well as news and giveaways.

VOLUME 2: A SPY IN THE DEEP

*I*f you enjoyed *The Dinosaur Hunters*, you can read more of Harriet's adventures in *A Spy in the Deep,* out now in ebook. It will also be released in November 2018 as a paperback.

≈

Mars, 1816

IF HARRIET GEORGE HAD EVER THOUGHT THAT TRAINING to become a spy would be easy, she had been disabused of that notion within a week. Spy training in the British-Martian Intelligence Service, it appeared, alternated between unending, droning lectures in poorly lit rooms and exercises in appalling danger and stupefying terror. Worse, Harriet never knew which she was in for when she arrived each morning.

When she had been recruited for the intelligence

service, she had been filled with confidence. And why not? She had been sixteen years old, had just solved the case of The Glass Phantom and the dinosaur hunters, *and* had caught a murderer. How hard could spy training be?

Within a week, she had realized that her previous success had been more down to luck than expertise. It had only been by chance that she hadn't been eaten alive by dinosaurs. Spy training was a lot harder than she'd expected. Sometimes, she winced remembering just how unprepared she'd been. That was when she wasn't wincing at the flying daggers, exploding booby traps, hideously murderous Martian creatures, and out-of-control clockwork mechanisms that made up a large part of her everyday lessons.

Now, almost a year later, everything seemed to be getting more difficult rather than easier. And none more so than her current exercise. She was crouched in a cramped, sweltering stone passageway trying – and failing – to disarm an absurdly complicated trap before she could be poisoned by gas, filleted by swords, swarmed by spear-spiders, or whatever delight awaited her today. She had solved the code scratched into the rock, aligned the dials, extracted the correct carved stone and reinserted it, but now the blasted lever WOULD NOT LIFT. A persistent ticking told her time was running out. Her hands were sweating, her hair was tangled across her face, and her dress was too tight around her chest. Why did she have to do this in a dress, anyway? The male trainees were free to wear trousers. Escaping from a hail of poisoned darts had to be easier in trousers.

"Come on," she whispered. "Come *on*."

A hand touched her lightly on the waist. Harriet jerked. Her hand twitched. The lever dropped. Harriet threw herself backwards, colliding with the person behind her.

A block of stone, which must have weighed several tons, smashed into the passageway, throwing up a cloud of dust and sand. Harriet coughed and furiously wiped her eyes clear.

"That," a voice said, "was the most pathetic display I have ever seen."

Harriet pushed herself up and twisted around. Reginald Pratt, Viscount Brotherton stood looking down at her, sneering.

"You blasted idiot!" Harriet exploded. "You could have killed me."

"Not if you knew what you were doing. But then, you're not much good at this, are you, George?"

Keep reading in the ebook A Spy in the Deep, out now, or in the paperback due out in November 2018.

THE "SECRETS OF THE DRAGON TOMB" SERIES

If you'd like to read more stories set in the same world, my SECRETS OF THE DRAGON TOMBS series takes you on further adventures to even stranger corners of the Mars. The novels feature different characters, but the same fun and adventure.

Book 1: Secrets of the Dragon Tomb

The year is 1816, the place is Mars. Home of pterodactyls, spies, and clockwork butlers...

All Edward Sullivan wants is to read his *Thrilling Martian Tales* in peace. But when a villainous archaeologist kidnaps his parents, Edward and his sisters must set out across the Martian wilderness to save them.

They'll have to dodge deadly beasts and murderous clockwork contraptions, and battle ruthless foes if they are to save their parents and uncover the secrets of the dragon tomb.

"Samphire's swashbuckling tale is both a pitch-perfect pastiche of a Victorian serial and a well-rounded, three-dimensional story of a boy learning that the world is more complicated than he thought. Abundant humor, intricate worldbuilding details, and precisely timed slapstick and mayhem mesh as neatly as the gears and

levers of the water abacus, producing a gorgeously articulated clockwork of a novel."

- Publishers Weekly (**Starred review**)

Book2: The Emperor of Mars

A missing Martian. A sinister plot. A French spy.

If Edward thought life was going to be easy in Tharsis City, he was very, very wrong. The moment he intercepts a thief escaping from Lady Harleston's townhouse, he is caught up in a terrible scheme that threatens the whole of Mars.

Soon he's fighting off vicious sea serpents, battling a small army of heavily-armored thugs, and trying to unpick an impossible mystery. Meanwhile, Putty has declared war on her new governess, a war that, for the first time in her life, Putty may be in danger of losing.

Edward doesn't know whom he can trust. Will he make the right choice? Or will his family – and his entire planet – fall victim to the treacherous Emperor of Mars?

"The sequel has all the puzzle solving, adventuring, and humor you remember from the first book but turned up a notch to make this read even better than the last!"

- YAYOMG!

ABOUT PATRICK SAMPHIRE

Patrick Samphire started writing when he was fourteen years old and thought it would be a good way of getting out of English lessons. It didn't work, but he kept on writing anyway.

He has lived in Zambia, Guyana, Austria, and England. He has been charged at by a buffalo and, once, when he sat on a camel, he cried. (He was young, all right. He was young!) Patrick has worked as a teacher, a physics journal editor and publisher, a marketing minion, and a pen pusher (real job!). Now, when he's not writing, he designs websites and book covers. He has a PhD in Theoretical Physics, which means that all the unlikely science in his books is actually true. Well, most of it. Well, some of it. Maybe.

Patrick now lives in Wales, U.K. with his wife, the awesome writer Stephanie Burgis, their two sons, and their cat. Right now, in Wales, it is almost certainly raining.

He has published almost twenty short stories in magazines and anthologies, including *Realms of Fantasy*, *Interzone*, *Strange Horizons*, and *The Year's Best Fantasy* as well as two novels, SECRETS OF THE DRAGON TOMB and THE EMPEROR OF MARS.

Made in the USA
Columbia, SC
05 May 2019